An American Story:
Uncollected Fiction

DANILO KIŠ

Translated and with an
Introduction by John K. Cox

AN AMERICAN STORY: UNCOLLECTED FICTION

DANILO KIŠ

Translated and with an
Introduction by John K. Cox

Translation and Introduction ©2016 John K. Cox
©2016 Szeged, AMERICANA eBooks

Chapters in this book are taken from Danilo Kiš, *Varia*, ed. by
Mirjana Miocinovic, Beograd: Prosveta, 2007. Copyrights for this
translation are courtesy of La Librairie Artheme Fayard

Crveni bik (*The Red Bull*), pp. 421-423
Juda (Odlomak), (*Judas, A Fragment*), pp. 424-430
Kosa (*The Hair*), pp. 431-434
Model (*The Model*), pp. 435-436
Galicija (*Galicia*), pp. 437-441
Zločin i kazna (*Crime and Punishment*), pp. 442-449
Cipele (*The Shoes*), pp. 450-455
Robot (*The Robot*), pp. 456-459
Bestiarium (*Bestiary*), pp. 460-463
Dečak s pticom na ramenu (*The Boy with a Bird on His Shoulder*), pp. 464-467
Kraj leta (*The End of Summer*), pp. 468-474
Američka prica (*An American Story*), pp. 475-481

ISBN 978-615-5423-27-7 (print); 978-615-5423-29-1 (mobi);
978-615-5423-28-4 (epub)

AMERICANA eBooks is a division of *AMERICANA – E-
Journal of American Studies in Hungary*, published by the
Department of American Studies,
University of Szeged, Hungary.
http://ebooks.americanaejournal.hu

Cover design by Kathleen T. Cox

CONTENTS

Introduction 1

The Red Bull 9

Judas (A Fragment) 11

The Hair 18

The Model 22

Galicia 25

Crime and punishment 30

The Shoes 38

The Robot 44

The Boy with a Bird on his Shoulder 49

A Bestiary 53

The End of the Summer 57

An American Story 64

INTRODUCTION

In the fall of 2014, I was teaching at the University of Szeged in southern Hungary as a Fulbright lecturer. Availing myself of the excellent fiction collections in that university's lovely and very modern library, I found three stories by Danilo Kiš that were new to me. This was only one of the exciting discoveries I made, with the help of many colleagues at the University, but it is important here because these three stories, from the later, expanded edition of *Varia*[1], deeply impressed me and, when combined with the other nine uncollected stories by Kiš about which I already knew, sparked my interest in looking for a way of bringing them all to an English-speaking audience.

I was very lucky that the University of Szeged contains an active and entrepreneurial Department of American Studies, and that this department maintains an academic journal and this press, AMERICANA eBooks. It seems a good match that this press should publish the translations of a visiting American academic, especially when one of the most prominent stories in the collection is set in the United States. This has really become an enthusiastic transnational project, with various kinds of input from

---

1 These three stories, "The Red Bull," "Galicia," and "The End of Summer" are found in the twelfth volume of Kiš's collected works, edited by Mirjana Miočinović. This volume is entitled *Varia* (Beograd: Prosveta, 2007). The other nine stories were already included in the earlier version of *Varia* (Beograd: BIGZ, 1995). These are the source versions used in this volume of translations.

Hungary, Serbia, and the United States. Proper commemoration of Kiš's life and work remains an ongoing concern. There is now a small statue of the man on the main square in his hometown of Subotica/Szabadka, but still no street, or other public place of institution, named after him there; Belgrade has a tiny street named after him, and Novi Sad, where he was baptized Orthodox and where he and his family nearly perished in the notorious massacres of 1942 known as the "Cold Days." There are streets named after him in Rumenka and other towns across Vojvodina, and a few schools bear his name in Montenegro, his mother's home province, where Kiš himself lived from 1947-1954.

It is also particularly fitting, I find, that a Hungarian press is bringing out this book. Right across the border from Szeged lies Subotica, an equally lovely, if smaller, Pannonian town that has been part of Yugoslavia since 1918; before the end of World War I, it was part of Hungary, which was in turn a part of the Habsburg Empire. It was in Subotica, or Szabadka, as the Hungarian half of his family would have called it, that Danilo Kiš was born; his father was a railroad inspector and the family lived near the tracks and administration buildings, close to what is today the international and long-distance bus depot.[2] But, in fact, the Hungarian connections to Kiš are a constant in his life. Trying to keep a low profile in the face of both German and Hungarian anti-semitism, Kiš's father Eduard took his wife, Milica, and their two children, Danilo and Danica, to the agricultural region in southwestern Hungary where he had grown up. Milica, Danica, and Danilo survived the war in miserable conditions, but Eduard did not. After several periods of forced labor and years of prejudice and persecution, he was rounded up and sent to the camps in 1944. Kiš

---

2 See Boško Krstić, *Potraga za Ulicom divljih kestenova: Subotičke uspomene (na) Danila Kiša.* 2nd ed. Subotica: Studio Bravo, 2007.

maintained an active interest in the Hungarian language and culture for the rest of his life, translating and reviewing many Hungarian publications, especially poetry, speaking Hungarian to certain friends, visiting Budapest and sites connected with his childhood, and building in many characters, landscapes, and artifacts from Hungary.

The stories in *An American Story: Uncollected Fiction* were originally published in the following sequence and in the following media:

Title of Story	Year of Publication	Journal or newspaper
The Red Bull	1953	*Susreti*
Judas	1954	*Susreti*
The Hair	1955	*Naša žena*
The Model	1955	*Susreti*
Galicia	1958	*Kadima*
Crime and Punishment	1959	*Mladost*
The Shoes	1960	*Delo*
The Robot	1961	*Pobjeda*
Bestiary	1962	*Književne novine*
Boy with a Bird on His Shoulder	1962	*Beogradska nedelja*
The End of Summer	1967	*Telegram*
An American Story	1967	*Jevrejski almanah*

By contrast, Kiš's other stories, most of which he formed into interconnected cycles or collections, began to appear in book form in 1970, with *Early Sorrows (For Children and Sensitive Readers)*. This was followed by the epoch-making *A Tomb for Boris Davidovich* (1976) and then *Encyclopedia of the Dead* (1983); *The Lute and the Scars* was a posthumous collection published in 1994. These works all exist already in English translations. The author's novels were published between 1962 and 1972; he also wrote a considerable amount in other genres, especially literary criticism and theory, and gave many lengthy interviews.

Today, little of Kiš's fiction remains to be translated. His unfinished novel, *Legenda o spavačima* (Eng. Legend of the Sleepers) is unbroached, but his autobiographical story "The Paris Trip" (orig. "Izlet u Pariz") will soon be appearing in the inaugural issue of the journal *Hourglass Literary Magazine*.[3] Of most immediate interest to readers of these stories, however, will likely be Kiš's set of three Joycean stories from 1959, "Mr. Poppy Enjoys Himself," "Mr. Poppy Takes a Walk," and "Noah's Ark (from Mr. Poppy's Notebook)." Mark Thompson gives in-depth analysis of these stories (alternately called essays or prose-poems) in his magisterial biography of Kiš,[4] where he had also included an excellent full translation of the third story.

Mirjana Miočinović, who edited and annotated both editions of the volume of Kiš's collected works entitled *Varia*, has provided the most important commentary on these stories. She stresses that in many of them, Kiš was "testing his own ear," as if he were a musician warming up by trying out his instrument and hitting the first few sample chords. Not surprisingly, she continues, in these stories

> are the shoots and sprouts of the later prose works, [and] their dominant themes..."Judas" (1954) precedes the entire family cycle, "The Hair" and "Galicia" prefigure *Psalm 44*, [and] "The Boy with a Bird on His Shoulder" and "Bestiary,"
> from 1962, are the first sketches for the novel *Garden Ashes*, the first—discarded, and justifiably—variations on the theme of "early sorrows."[5]

---

3 See www.hourglassonline.org.

4 This award-winning and already oft-translated volume, which is profound, engaging, and sympathetic to Kiš, is *Birth Certificate: The Story of Danilo Kiš* (Ithaca, NY: Cornell University Press, 2013). Thompson is an accomplished scholar of twentieth-century Yugoslav history and also possesses keen literary insights and inexhaustible knowledge of the Serbian cultural scene.

5 Mirjana Miočinović, "Pogovor," in Danilo Kiš, *Varia* (Beograd: Prosveta, 2007), 567.

Three other stories, "Crime and Punishment," "The Robot," "The End of Summer," and "An American Story" show the influence of Croatian literary giant Miroslav Krleža; written in the third person, with a large quotient of dialogue, they are "anecdotes at their core" and represent a style Kiš soon left behind.[6] The "complete literary program" of these stories is completed by "The Shoes," which Miočinović calls an "extended echo of *The Attic*" and a novelization of Kiš's "theory of (his future) prose, the intuitive theory of defamiliarization, or *ostranenie*."[7] Most concretely Kiš was learning at this time the importance of "distance and irony" and of braking his "sentimentality, pathos, and uncontrolled lyricism."[8] This distance for which he eventually and so successfully opted included, after the novel *Psalm 44*, a diminished role for graphic descriptions of atrocity and, some would argue, a heightened awareness of humor at times.

Readers of these stories will certainly notice their wide range of subject matter and style. Fully five of them, nearly half of the collection, deal with the Holocaust, the catastrophe that not only shaped Kiš's life, artistic ethos, and the subject matter of his writings for much of his career. The most unusual of these is "Crime and Punishment," a kind of totalitarian fable that gives up many of its truths only after several readings. "The Boy with a Bird on His Shoulder" is arguably the finest story in this book. It rings true in ways we do not want it to, and its evocation of childhood is void of sentimentality but fertile in emotion and dread; Kiš's ear for the necessarily laconic conversation is breathtakingly, masterfully precise. The protagonist in "Galicia" displays a quiet emotional

---

6 Miočinović, "Pogovor 2007," 567.
7 Mirjana Miočinović, "Pogovor," in Danilo Kiš, *Varia* (Beograd: BIGZ, 1995), 579-580.
8 Miočinović, "Pogovor 2007," 567.

generosity and maturity that belie his age but are perfectly calibrated and authentic.

Two of Kiš's other common themes, namely the vulnerability of the outsider, and its corollary, variations on the embodiment of the Other, are well represented here as well. In fact, almost every one of the stories can be viewed from that vantage point. "The Robot" is as clear and clever a depiction of the fuzzy line between "us" and "them" as one could wish for.

With regard to form and style, there are also noteworthy experimentations among these tales. Altered perspectives and musings on the relation of form to reality impart the intellectual heft to "The Red Bull" and "The Shoes." If there is surrealism in Kiš's work, or even a touch of science fiction, it is to be found above all in "The Model" and "The End of Summer," a work also notable for its sense of Mediterranean place and history. In the original Serbo-Croatian, "The Red Bull" reads as lyrically and as modestly as a mature poem, and "Bestiary," combining (again) pointillist conversation with sun-splashed, fragile, expectant memories of childhood, achieves an unsurpassed purity of vision and emotional force in its three brief but close-grained pieces.

There is good reason that we have had no reason to discuss the political background to these works that originated, and were first published, in a communist (or socialist) country. By the time Kiš began writing, the Communist Party of Yugoslavia had changed its name to the League of Communists of Yugoslavia, and started to reduce its commanding presence in the society; the country had left the Soviet bloc, allowing a political evolution towards a "third path" between Moscow and Washington; and intellectuals had already joined the battle against dogmatism, socialist realism, or instrumentalization of art in cultural spheres.[9] In other words, Yugoslav

9 Yugoslavia's unique medial position in the Cold War, and its

communist authorities were by this time, the mid-1950s, on their way to the point where they censored, prosecuted, or persecuted the country's artists only in extreme cases, where public morality or socialist historiography or iconography (or the political order itself, of course) was seen to be under attack.[10] But it is also true that Kiš had bigger fish to fry than politics. His concern, taking shape in his art and through the point of view of his own family, was history, or lived politics, as he might have said. Before he overtly took up cudgels against communism in the 1970s, the history that suffused his work was the history that he had lived through as a child. His reading, translating, and multifarious intellectual influences of course provided him with numerous avenues of literary growth and experimentation. But in the story "Judas (A Fragment)," we are confronted with the enormity of the tasks Kiš was just setting himself: how to write across linguistic, religious, regional, and ethnic lines; how to honor or redeem his family's suffering amidst competing demands of childhood memories and the ruin of Central European culture; and how to evoke a sense of place in which the mud and restriction of Central Europe contrast very unfavorably with the limitless light and possibility of the nearby sea.

---

fragmented demographic landscape, made it very difficult for cultural dogmatists to impose anything akin to "socialist realism," a Stalinist or Zhdanovite manipulation of cultural production and interpretation, in the country. That said, Kiš, and many since him, railed against the constraints of the "critical realism" or "socialist aestheticism" that valorized the League of Communists' interpretation of history and left artists susceptible to nationalism and impervious to innovation. See Sveta Lukić, *Contemporary Yugoslav Literature: A Sociopolitical Approach*, trans. Pola Triandis (Urbana, IL: University of Chicago Press, 1972).

10 These persecutions could be vicious, and of long duration, but when compared to those of Yugoslavia's communist neighbors, they were fewer in number, and Yugoslavs also had a much easier time traveling or emigrating.

***

This translation was greatly aided by assistance from the following people: Irén Annus, Patrick Apić, Tamara Vujanić Apić, Dušan Bogdanović, Nina Jovanović, Bea Klotz, Boško Krstić, Ivan Nador, Jeff Pennington, Dragan Miljković, Pete Stokić, Róbert Túri, and Thomas Williams. Delightful and knowledgeable people all, I'm lucky to know them. Warm thanks go also to my wife, Kathleen Turley Cox, for the captivating cover design.

Without the generosity and wisdom of Pascale Delpech and Mirjana Miočinović, this project would not have been possible; I owe them a great deal. And without the work of Réka M. Cristian, Zoltán Dragon, and Véronique Heron, this book would never have been published, and I would like to express my gratitude to each of them.

This translation is dedicated to my friends Linda Kúnos and András Dávid, whose reliable intellectual guidance, curiosity, tolerance, and tremendous big-city hospitality have meant so much to me over the years.

John K. Cox (john.cox.1@ndsu.edu)

THE RED BULL

People were gathering around, jostling each other, growing agitated. I was near the tracks. The open arena stretched out before me. My skin was crawling, as if a corpse were reaching out to me with its icy touch. A few steps in front of me lay a hunk of meat—it resembled brains or a lung—which looked as though it had just fallen from the basket of a clumsy housewife. The crowd swelled and churned towards the street light like reeds in a bog. From an adjacent café came the sounds of a waltz, enticing but somehow sad, too.

"She jumped by herself. By God, it's no one's fault but her own..." My ears caught that, and I started to listen in.

"I would have treated her with love! Sixteen years old, and such scandal!"

"Look! 900-dinar sandals—" said one girl behind me, pointing beneath the streetcar.

A boy inquired: "Did she have nice legs at least?" At that, everyone standing around him smiled.

"Suicide. Girl. Fifteen or sixteen—" shot into my consciousness.

And then, along the tracks, I made out pieces of meat: here some brains, there some scalped brown hair in locks, a little farther along a leg, squished beneath the wheels but still fitted with a petite red sandal...I studied that leg for a long time, and those little red sandals. I felt ashamed, as if I were looking at her naked. I felt suffocated under my tears, but I started to pull apart my lips to try to smile—so that I'd be similar in every way to the people around me. I turned away, but I felt as though I were lagging behind the others, and I started to laugh, at first softly, and then in peals of angry guffawing, right up to the point I made myself deaf with my own cries—so I wouldn't hear the laughter of the others all around.

Here and there uniforms were ferociously standing up to the crowd that had constricted around them...

I felt as though I had fallen into an arena. In front of me lay the mangled *toreador*, while the red bull—the streetcar—looked at him triumphantly with his phosphorous yellow eyes...

All of a sudden, the red bull started to rear, and beneath its bloody feet something was moving, something square, bloody, disfigured. I noticed, in the chaos of meat, blood, bones, and dress...oh, why did I have to see that?...I noticed breasts...No, they weren't breasts. This wasn't beauty, passion, or debauchery; this was a secret, long preserved and hidden forever, innocence sullied by blood and motor oil, by watching eyes and laughter—it was the irony of youth and beauty!

The body (better: meat) they stuffed into a sack. The red sandals were no longer in their place. There was just music playing, more and more powerful and mesmerizing. People giggled and beamed, and the timid beating of the bass drum, the snare, and the cymbals, the howls of the trombone, the hopping of the violin—all of it resembled applause for the red bull who had triumphed, and it resembled booing and hissing at the bloody *toreador*, his humiliated body impotent and butchered...

The crowd began melting away, the front rows first, while the others, dissatisfied at not having seen the meat, started sniffing around the tracks—at least they'd get to see blood! The wheels of the streetcar lurched into motion with a clatter...the applause died away...and in the distance were the fading sounds of a waltz.

(1953)

JUDAS (A FRAGMENT)

When the worm-eaten door to his room squeaked open, he was welcomed by deafening silence. The woman lay on the low bed with her eyes squeezed shut. It was full of bedbugs, and she was paler than ever. The children stared out the window at the farmhouse, goggle-eyed but resentful, and sluggish. Silence. No one greeted him with a "Good day," no one came to meet him, and no one even looked at him. They were communicating in the language of misfortune. He knew they'd all been eagerly waiting for him, impatiently, consoling their empty bellies with the thought of his imminent return. He had gone to pick up his pay. He was bringing them bread. Or maybe something more than just bread, since it was, people said, a holiday. (Everybody's kids were dressed up, breaking open colored Easter eggs and eating poppy-seed pastries.)

They saw him when he was still far off, walking with his head down, slowly, like a person at a funeral. (But today is Easter—and no one has died!) And now everyone is quiet—as if he had not even come in. They were ashamed to look at him. He knew they'd heard him, despite his quiet entrance. He knew that his wife wasn't sleeping and that she saw the neck of the bottle protruding from his pocket...Every unnecessary glance would sting them in their misery, which was more powerful than any words could convey. But beneath her darkened eyelids he saw the illness in the eyes of his wife, and he saw the fatigued look on the faces of his starving children. Truth be told, his insides were also knotted with hunger, but he didn't hear the persistent drumming of empty guts, for it was overpowered by the ridiculous cannonade of his defective nerves.

So now he stood there, helpless, trembling in every capillary and nerve. That very morning he had come to an ominous realization, and now he regarded his family the way a suicide case looks at himself in the mirror for the last time: with a revolver at his temple. And yet he still had enough strength in him to be capable of bursting out in tears, and to register pain, but everything else was done—he had passed judgment on himself.

After stubbornly and pointlessly roaming the city on a search for something to make his sick, famished family happy, he found himself in a tavern—without even knowing how or when he got there. "Drink up! It's the elixir of life!" a voice whispered to him. It was demonic; it spoke insistently and irresistably. And he could not resist it. He sat down on the one bench in the wall and ordered *rakija*, then wine, then *rakija*...

And all of a sudden, the whole world was wonderful, bright, and wide-open.

In a corner of the tavern there were Roma playing a manic csardas, the whole place was wobbling, and all the people were shouting and clinking glasses and toasting the risen Christ—and round and round it all spun in Kohn's inebriated brain, like a garish merry-go-round on market day.

Eventually he rose up, as readily as a somnambulist, like someone freed from the laws of gravity. His briefcase, which he usually kept firmly in his grasp, he had left on the bench, while the yellow star, with its six points and its blood-like streaks of wine, flashed on his chest.

Then came a cry from someone in the crowd. They were pointing at him with their fingers, guffawing, mocking.

There he is. *Judas*! Get him over here! He's the one who—who crucified Christ!

These words had a magical effect on the pack. In a moment the music had stopped, the voices died out, and everyone's eyes were fixed on the drunken Mr. Kohn. In each member of the crowd a gladiatorial lust came to life—and they initiated a cruel game. Immediately a living ring took shape around him: unruly, intoxicated people, dousing him with wine, spitting on him, laughing at him and his shitty yellow symbol, and then the Roma resumed their rousing *csárdás*, with violins shrieking, cymbals bashing, and the contrabass groaning.

> *I'd give everything*
> *Give all I have*
> *For those lying eyes*
> *For those oh, oh, oh!*

Everything was spinning, and it went to Kohn's head and filled it with manic confusion—but he only felt one thing: that they had offended him!

"Who? He crucified Christ?...But wasn't Christ a Jew?"

"Hey, maestro! Play that one of ours...We...(Ptui! Someone spat right into the middle of his face)...We Jews...I'll pay! That one of ours:

> *Tumbala*
> *tumbala*
> *tumbalaleika."*

Éljen Szálasi! someone who was three sheets to the wind called out excitedly.

Éljeeeeeeen!—the crowd takes up this cry with what seems like a hundred voices and drowns out Kohn's chosen hymn.

Out of malice someone commands the Gypsies to interrupt their *csárdás* and begin singing, with instrumental accompaniment:

Long live Szálasi
and his papa, too—
they toss nooses
round the necks of the Jews.

After that they broke out in a march of Jewish slaves. It was an alcohol-fueled mockery. A paroxysm of anti-Semitism:

The march rings out,
and then the command
kikes pushing barrows
in a gangster band.

And Kohn's head was swimming. Only one thing out of all the chaos reached his mind, one painful realization: they were insulting him! Spitting all over him and his star—all in the name of Christ and in praise of Szálasi...And after he fretted and gesticulated in his seat for a long time, denying, protesting, muttering drunkenly and inarticulately, he abruptly exploded in bestial screams. He shouted down the entire tavern with his ox-like bass voice. the people all paused, in order to hear what he might say. He showed them how his late father distinguished Tokay from swill—simply by sipping it and then spitting it out forthwith, never swallowing a drop; brought up some five thousand-year old sufferings; displayed tearfully his wine-covered star, convincing them all that the knife-wound in his heart had provided the stains. He explained all of these things amidst the debauchery and chaos, as he was teased and egged on from all sides.

The whole paschal uproar in the inn concluded with Kohn—after he had burnt through all his pay—being tossed out like a suitcase into the drainage trench in front. They grabbed him, battered and covered in sputum, by the arms and legs and—heave, ho!—out he went through the door, without his briefcase, without his hat. Throwing a

Jew out the doors of a watering hole into the gutter of a filthy street had an enormous amount of symbolism connected with it, and it originated as a natural continuation of the morning's Easter mass, from the celebration of which many of the patrons in the bar had come.

Thus Kohn lay on his back in the reeking ditch, thrashed and muddied. Blood poured from his nose across his face and ran across that yellow star of his, sewn from the silk of a quilt and now marked with spit, mud, and blood...And the star lay together with him in the polluted municipal drainage ditch.

He spent a few hours sleeping like this, a dead, wasted sleep, like that of a bloated cur that has croaked in the ditch and been washed down to this spot. He then extricated himself with great difficulty and set off for home, whipped and lost.

And now, avoiding the others' glances in the unpleasant atmosphere, he looks through the window. A Lucullan feast is in preparation at his relatives' home in the farmhouse.

The sun of the April afternoon descended softly over the muscat-ringed patio, and the polyp-like creatures crept out of their dusky nesting grounds—to sun themselves. Everyone is present; everybody is decked out for the holiday, provocatively loud and nonchalant. In the center of the patio, a table: multi-colored Easter eggs, a cake with a wax candle in it, pastries, wine, *rakija*. Everyone is snickering, clinking glasses, drinking, smacking their lips, belching. And after eating, they all make themselves comfortable. Netty (his sister), who is now dizzier than usual on account of drink, has parked herself in a chair and is stuffing nuts into an already fat turkey. The turkey is choking, gasping, and giving a death rattle like a drowning victim while she clutches it tightly with her hands and knees and crams handfuls of shelled walnuts down its throat. His niece, Mrs. Berki, reads the Easter prayer in a quiet voice, mumbling repeatedly that—all men are brothers. Mr. Berki, her husband, relaxing on a sofa, is reading *The Captain of the Silver Bell* by Jack Mecklern (whom he calls Jack). He pours more wine after every page and sips it in his blissful reptilian way.

Mr. Berki's sons are making a fuss over their *relative*. The older one was holding her in his lap (where her skirt—accidentally—worked its way far up above her freckled knees), while the younger one, eyes gleaming, watched on in wonderment. And her cross-eyed breasts quivered like rabbits beneath the broad palms with which he covered them, while her watery blue eyes emitted the sly, promiscuous glow that made the others tremble in drunken heat.

The whole crowded scene spun before Kohn's eyes— just like back in the tavern. He watched them as if he were half-asleep, pondering nonetheless how insolent and provocative it all was. None of them thought to inquire of him how things were in his "apartment,"—as they referred to the horse stalls in which he lodged—or whether his children had anything to eat. Although everyone could see that his wife was sick and unable to get around...

And all at once it seemed to Kohn that he had to do something immediately—otherwise he would explode! For all these things were unbearable and illogical. Outside—the luxurious sun and the whirling expanse of the day, while in his room—everything smelled of the horse piss that had sunk into the moist, stamped earth. Everything smelled of misery, poverty.

He was suffocating!

And, not letting the motley, repulsive crowd out of his sight, he drew the bottle out of his pocket, slowly, the way a killer pulls out his revolver—and he brought its mouth up to his lips. None of his family members were looking at him. The potent brandy left an agreeable feeling of heat in his throat, and it spread throughout his being right to the tips of his toes. It coursed through every vein, every capillary, and abruptly—Boom!—something snapped inside him like an overtightened string. Out of control, he grabbed the nearly empty bottle, kept it away from his lips, with tremendous effort, like a hungry child being separated from its mother's breast, and with a forceful swing of his arm hurled it through the window at the swarming pack. Afterwards he shrieked, with his final ounce of strength, in such a terrible, mad voice that the whole house began to shake:

"That house belonged to *my father*! I will not allow people to carry on in it like this! I

won't!...I won't...I....!"

And, as if he were plunging from the gallows, he collapsed in a helpless pile, broken by hunger

and by suffering.

(1954)

THE HAIR

All that remained of her earlier beauty was her hair. Her long hair, red as copper.

The first to fall was the tall girl, who slid along in front of her across the superheated sheet metal, carefully dragging her bucket of paint. They all ran frantically towards her, down the flimsy ladder, but the guards drove them back. From then on, the ladders were only in place when the women were going up or down them. Now they would hear a shriek but they wouldn't turn around.

Early one morning, they were stuffed into trucks and driven somewhere far away. Then, like a religious procession clad in gray, they climbed, one after the other, into the dizzying heights with the baking sun, where they proceeded to cover the factory's roof with green paint.

Some of them were falling from exhaustion. But some were voluntarily giving themselves over to the embrace of nothingness, the void.

And now they were going to wrest from her that one treasure, the copper and living gold, by which she could still tell herself apart from these other woman, distinguish herself among these numbers. It was the only feature that let her remember her name, which was being crowded out of her mind by a number.

They stood in long rows, wearing workers' overalls, smeared with green paint. The duty officer read off an order: for reasons of hygiene, all women in the camp must have their hair shorn.

Everyone held her long hair against her, but she was proud of her tresses. And Henri had told her that he loved her precisely because of her hair, and that without it she wouldn't be herself, and he wouldn't be able to recognize her.

"What's this, beautiful?" the commandant said, mocking her. He had his hand on her chin and pushed up her head.

She kept quiet and watched him through the fine prism of her tears, looking at him like a little girl, although she didn't want to do so. She wanted to blurt something offensive into his face.

"Report to me in the office, at once," he barked at her.

If only she could preserve her hair for Henri, she could one day spill all this treasure into his lap and see it set him aflame, her red torch. Someday, when they were married, and when there was no more war.

"Yes, it's certainly tough to have to sacrifice hair like this," the camp commandant said. He reached out with his hand, but she recoiled and evaded his touch.

"You are ungrateful, my little beauty," said the commandant. "But see here. I am prepared to help you. We'll transfer you, upon my personal intercession, into the administration. That way we can save your hair," he said, and he moved toward her.

"Don't touch me. Don't pollute this, you—" she lashed out at him. Then she rushed, panic-stricken, to the door. The door was locked. She felt horror and looked helplessly at the commandant.

"Ha, ha, you are saving your hairy for Henri," he said with a laugh. "You see? We know everything."

Someone knocked on the door. The commandant walked over, pulled out his key, and opened up. She ran out, skirting the soldier who was clicking his heels. She heard, as if from the remoteness of a dream:

"I'm giving you fifteen minutes, No. 2071; (Yes, I heard my name correctly); think it over—I'm sending the barber your way."

How did the commandant know about Henri? He compromised himself, didn't he, by registering with a Jew like her? Perhaps he had written to her, or come looking for her?

She sat down on the hard bed in her room and picked up her mess kit. But she quickly put it back down again. She knew that these were spontaneous motions, just as she had known spontaneously that it was time for lunch. Hunger is no way to measure time.

She was getting ready for her first public appearance. Henri brought her a newspaper: starting tomorrow, every Jewish man and woman must wear a yellow six-pointed star. She sewed one onto her black evening gown and took a seat at the piano. She played Liszt. All of a sudden she noticed the audience leaving the hall. She walked home weeping and spent a long time washing her breasts and her hair. With scorn or in sympathy they had all kept their eyes directed at her delicate nipples for a long time He had been the only one to console her—by caressing her breasts and hair.

"The commandant wants to know whether we are to give the young lady a haircut?" the barber said. He was clacking his scissors.

But what was Henri going to say when he saw her without hair? She knew she was now gaunt and swarthy from exposure to sun and dank air, just as she knew of the withering of her bosom where the yellow star had once proudly stood out.

"Cut it," she said. Or she merely thought it.

She heard the slicing of the scissors, stiff and painful, as if they were cutting into living flesh. Two bunches of red hair fell into her lap from the barber's hand, and she felt as if her hands had been amputated. Then the man ran the electric shaver across her head, and hair poured into her lap like blood from her throat, like fallen and withered leaves.

She touched her head. It was the caress of a young hedgehog making desperate motions in the sun.

She picked up her withered tresses and stroked them. She recognized herself again; she remembered her name. Then she started to braid the fallen hair, thinking back to what it was like to be close to Henri, recalling his hands as they stroked her, remembering herself, herself as pretty, as a redhead, herself as his, as her past self.

He loved to play with her curls. To wrap them around her neck and squeeze her throat with this beautiful lasso until she drained his strength through kisses. Then he would uncoil the embrace from her throat and kiss her there, as if he had just laid eyes on the pale skin of her neck for the first time.

Why had the barber not told her before the shearing that Henri was waiting for her? That was certainly the commandant's revenge. She felt as though she really needed to show herself today to Henri today with her hair. Because one day she too would fall headfirst from the roof of the factory. It was unavoidable. So why should she on that day stay lodged in his memory like this: shorn and ugly. She would have given anything to know that Henri was waiting for her. And to avoid profaning this one memory, the memory of herself.

In front of the gate to the Jewish women's camp, a man walked back and forth impatiently. He was smoking a cigarette. When the truck carrying the male workers went past, he said nothing. He was waiting for the women to show up.

In the early evening the guard informed him:

"Prisoner No. 2071 is no longer on the list."

(1955)

THE MODEL

The first thing she did was remove her red shawl. Then she draped her coat on a hanger next to the podium where she would be posing. She slid off her dress; its fabric was colorful. And there she stood, with all her limbs exposed, wearing only a slip. Without even stooping she flung the tiny shoes from her feet and all at once even her lower legs were bare. In one more sure and rapid movement the last little piece of clothing was up and gone, and nothing was left covering her lustrous nakedness.

The sculptor followed every movement of his mannequin, but he did so with indifferent eyes. He gave her some instructions on how to pose—pose in such a way as to give expression to all the sensuality of a young woman.

Then he started mixing the clay with his fingers, started making shapes. And the model in front of him began to turn white. First her entire body took on a spectral shade of pale. After that he noticed every movement of her limbs, and even of her muscles, taper off. He was amazed, but only at how a dead body could remain on its feet in such an impossible position, with its arms thrown back behind its head and its chest thrust upward. He saw that she had stopped blinking and was staring vaguely out into space with the eyes of a corpse. Before those eyes he lowered his gaze; his trembling hands created forms in the wet clay and made casts of plaster. At that point she stopped breathing. The gleam went out of her eyes all at once, her pupils disappeared somewhere up and under her

22

lids, and her lashes dried out like pine needles. The sculptor paused and just stood there; he looked panic-stricken. Then he picked up a mirror and took it over to her half-open lips, barren and cold. The mirror did not fog over. Then he touched her, with his palm, beneath her upraised left breast. She was as cool and firm as chiselled white marble, and his hand failed to detect any hint of life. Her heart was not beating.

Now perspiration ran down over his face. He thought he'd try to find a pulse on her left arm and so he quickly grabbed her by the wrist. He noticed at once that the arm simply fell; it was dead, snapped off above the elbow. But no blood came gushing out of the rupture. He let her arm drop and it struck the ground with a thud. There it lay, unmoving. Cautiously he felt for a pulse on her right arm. His touch must have been barely perceptible. But the arm came loose immediately and fell as if from a skeleton. He wanted to close her eyelids, because the whites of her eyes were bulging horribly. But her head began to rock to and fro and then it tumbled to the floor as though it were a mere skull.

What he had before him was a torso. The plaster on the bulges of her raised breasts had grown white and now it shone with heightened sensualness.

It was only when he beheld her adjusting her garters, when he saw the delicate little bumps on the skin of her breasts, when clothing covered her thighs and waist—it was only then that he realized that what he had before him was a woman. It was a woman with a body, a woman of flesh and blood. And when he paid her the honorarium for posing, she took the money from his hands and left behind the warm touch of her fingers.

He heard her high heels resounding in the hallway. He could see, through her sheer stockings, the graceful curve of her legs. Then all at once, as soon as she was lost from view, he felt his arm burning where she had touched him;

he knew his head was spinning now from the warmth of her breath. It was her eyes that had set his heart to racing.

Exhaling, he felt intoxicated: it was the scent of a woman's body that hovered now in the air of his studio like a misty veil of white.

(1955)

GALICIA

When he reached the Plaza, it was past midnight. Subsequently he slowed his pace, for it made no sense at all to hurry. The bus had already left anyway, and the next one wasn't due to depart for another hour.

He went down the steep street leading from the Square. He loved these little streets after midnight, when they were nearly empty. That's why it disturbed him when the boys, who came running around the corner of the street he named the Street of Goodbyes, laughed so loudly. Andreas pressed himself against the wall to let them pass. He didn't want them to ruin the quiet of this street. They didn't notice him. Behind them wobbled, on drunken legs, a man, evidently with the intention of catching up to them. But when he saw Andreas, who was crossing the street on the sly, the man turned to him:

"You tink ze German iss crazy. Ze German iss not crazy. Jess drunk."

The boy walked on without turning to meet his gaze. But the man blocked his path.

"So do you tink ze German iss crazy?"

Andreas thought: Here's a way to kill that hour. And he said:

"It'd be best if you went home to bed. You could get arrested."

"D'you have a cigarette?" the man asked.

"Here," the boy said, offering him the pack. They both lit up.

"You must be a student," the man remarked after a moment.

"Yes," said Andreas. They were walking quietly along the Street of Goodbyes.

Without speaking they had descended into a men's room.

The man said: "Well, I'm a painter. Not the ordinary kind, not houses. I'm an artist, mind you."

"Why do you drink?" asked Andreas as they left the bathroom. The man shrugged his shoulders.

"I regret," he stated, "that I'm not in a position to stand you a round. But I could talk to you about Galicia...But it's not like you'd know where that is, right?"

"I know," the boy said.

They reached the Café Paris, and Andreas looked through the window. It was almost empty.

"I'd like it if you told me about Galicia," the boy said. "Let's duck in here. I could use a glass of wine." Then he turned the pockets of his corduroy trousers inside out.

"I gather you know where Galicia is?" the man asked once they had taken their seats in a corner.

"I know," the young man replied.

"I was in a concentration camp there," the man went on.

"A concentration camp?"

"Yes," the man said. "I was, you know a guard. A *Volksdeutscher.* I'll bet you definitely don't know what a *Volksdeutscher* is."

"Oh, I know,' the boy said. And then, after he'd ordered wine: "Why didn't you go back home?"

"Ah. There's nobody there for me," the man said.

"Killed?"

"Yes."

Then the boy said:

"Tell me about Galicia."

The man drank his wine, and Andreas smoked cigarette after cigarette.

"Galicia, Galicia, if I could but see Galicia," the man said, grinding out his cigarette butt in the ashtray.

"Are you from Galicia?" the boy asked.

"No," the man answered. "That's where the camp was where I worked as a guard. There were lots of Jews there, you know."

Now the man stopped talking. The boy abruptly broke the silence:

"From all over the world," Andreas added, as if he were continuing the man's thoughts.

"I'm sorry to be using up all your cigarettes."

"Never mind. Take more," the boy said.

He looked at the prostitute who was staggering along beside the bar.

"I was in love with a Jewish woman from Odessa," the man blurted out. The boy was no longer looking at the prostitute.

"She had beautiful, delicate hands..." the man added.

The woman behind the bar noticed that the boy was looking at her again and she grinned idiotically at him.

"We would meet in secret," the man said. "My friend Hans helped us. The first time I saw her, I took pity on her, although I had already seen enough to become hardened. And I fell in love with her. Later I would secretly take her sugar and bread."

The woman had now ascended a tall stool near the bar and crossed her legs. Then a man wearing a blue laborer's jacket took a seat next to her.

"So, what happened to her, your Jewish lady?" asked the boy, who was pretending to take no special interest in the man's story.

"They killed her when they found out I had been visiting her, and I was sent to the front. I almost bought it there."

The boy hadn't noticed it when the prostitute left the café. Aside from the two of them, guests were now few and far between. All around them chairs had already been turned upside down and placed atop the tables.

"It's late," the boy said. He paid. "I need to go home. Shall we look for each other here tomorrow? What time are you off?"

"I'm always off," the man said.

"I mean, when do you work?"

"Oh, I don't have a job," the man continued.

"Just sometimes when they call me in. But I drink up everything around me and they have to give me the sack."

"What do you live off of?" the young man inquired. The man shrugged his shoulders.

They were standing on a corner, trying to shield themselves from the wind. Abruptly the man said:

"Look." And he unbuttoned his gray work tunic.

"I don't even have a shirt. I don't have anything. (And I don't need anything.) It's easy now, but soon it will be winter."

"Well, where do you live?" the boy wanted to know.

"Nowhere," the man replied. "I sleep under the bridge or in the café, until they throw me out. As you can see, I don't even have a shirt."

"Here's mine," the boy announced and started unbuttoning his jacket. "I have another."

"No," the man interrupted. "How can you go home without your shirt?"

"That's true. How would that look...? Do you want to get together tomorrow? I'll bring you a different one. In front of the Paris at 11 in the evening?"

"Tomorrow at 11 pm," the man repeated. "I'll come. You'll bring me a shirt. I'll talk to you about Galicia again...I mean, I know you don't even know where that is."

"I know, I know,' the boy said as he thought: what would it be like if I told him... that somewhere in Galicia...

The two of them had to get off the sidewalk because the street washers had arrived. The water rushed down the steep incline, carrying cigarette butts and wilted leaves.

Andreas' feet got wet through his sandals. He offered the German a cigarette, and, while he was lighting up, he looked at his unshaven face. These were his last two cigarettes. He threw the empty pack out onto the asphalt, where the jet from the rubber hose carried it off in no time at all. He then watched as the empty pack floated downhill, the stream of water flowing to places it had not reached before.

(1958)

CRIME AND PUNISHMENT

The jury consisted of Gavro, Hitler, and Oleg. They were seated on the podium. Close by, on a three-legged stool to their left, crouched the defendants. And in front of the jury, like the *corpus delicti*, placed on a crumpled handkerchief on which the blood was already dry: one heavy boot, a half-eaten piece of "American" cheese, some cut-up pages from old newspapers.

Everyone sat there in silence. Hitler rolled a cigarette, and after two or three puffs he passed it on to Gavro. And Gavro to Oleg. After the jury, the cigarette made its way into the hands of the defense. From somewhere off to the left some kind of commotion could be heard now and then, accompanied by the screeching of the voices of mice.

All of a sudden someone whispered under his breath: "Psssst. Shift change." But still all one could hear was the squeaking. In a bit someone on the outside scratched on the door with a toenail. They heard somebody flipping through a set of keys and then carefully inserting a key into the lock.

"Ready?" Tomahawk inquired, locking the door behind him.

"We're all set!" said someone from the jury.

Asclepius—he was representing the defense—then took his place alongside the accused and produced a grubby little notebook. Hitler was in charge of the proceedings. It appeared that he knew his way around the law. He was seated in the middle, between Gavro and Oleg.

"We can begin, gentlemen," Hitler said in a low, solemn voice. He picked up some handwritten files from the table. "The accused—" (his voice was hoarse) was how he began, and he filled the cell with dread. He spoke in moderate and formal tones, referring to sections and subsections of law, to justice and morality, and now and again he would take a peek at his files, something that lent him even more authority. Everyone was in awe of his erudition.

Outside the door, steps could be heard from time to time. Then the juror would lower his voice to a whisper, but without interrupting his presentation. Only the defendants would continue to act unconstrained. As if out of spite.

The indictment was read by de Coto. As he was walking up to the podium (two chairs with a bed across them), it became obvious, from his echoing steps, that he had a limp. He put his hand out towards the "Bible" (Tomahawk had procured somewhere or other an old church calendar for 19**, a leap year) and declared, with his eyes on the low ceiling:

"I swear."

"Are you sticking by your statement?"

"I demand, o illustrious court, the most severe penalty?" de Coto said. His voice was shaking. Gavro and Oleg looked at each other and nodded their heads.

And then came the examination of witnesses.

De Coto took two or three steps to the left (the light in the cell was dim), cast a quick glance toward the defendants, returned to his original place, and said: "Illustrious Court, and Your Honor the judge, there is no doubt: they are the ones." He could pick them out of a line-up of hundreds. "We lived together for years." And then he told the whole story from the beginning. How at the start they were friends—brothers, and more than brothers—how they shared everything (save the cigarettes; they don't smoke, you know). Everything: from crusts of bread to the "American" cheese. How later his trust was abused. Then the thievery and deception began, and continued, until finally they were plotting against his life, and then he'd had enough. He set a trap for them, and..."You know the rest," he said, shifting his weight from one foot to the other.

"No one was conspiring to kill him," Asclepius maintained. "But they were plotting to get his leg. That's what infuriated him." Laughter in the room.

"The defense will have the floor in turn," Hitler said sternly, and the laughing died away.

Then the defense had the floor.

"Gentlemen of the jury, Your Honor," Asclepius began, somewhat uncertainly. "I object. Ob-jec-tion." A hush fell over the room. "I would request of the Illustrious Court, before you retire and have your say and deliver a just verdict, that you hearken to the words of the defense. Ahem. Since my wards are not (and this is totally understandable) in a position to present information in their own defense or do anything to ameliorate their situations, permit me in their name to—"

"Get to the point!" someone heckled.

"Very well, Illustrious Court," Asclepius continued angrily. "It will not be necessary for me to take up too much of your time convincing the court that the charges against my clients are inflated and malicious and—most importantly—inaccurate. For (first off): it is not true that my clients did all these things with premeditation. Rather it was in the heat of the moment and, so to speak, out of ignorance. We are all, Your Honor, killers. Now, look here—I will mention only the fact that I am a prosecutor myself, as everyone knows..."

"Shut up, you back-stabbing asshole," de Coto snapped.

"... Everyone knows I am a prosecutor myself—I said—despite twelve years already served for murder..."

"Back-stabbing asshole! Asshole!" de Coto shouted menacingly and got to his feet.

"Quiet! Quiet!" Oleg rapped lightly on the plank with his palm.

"We will have to clear the hall if—"

"They'll hear us, and we'll all end up in solitary, you morons...The trial will continue. The defense has the floor."

"As I said, Your Honor, we are all murderers."

"Or thieves!" someone heckled.

"Or two-timing jerk-offs," de Coto hissed.

"It makes no difference, sir. Backstabbers, thieves, or murderers—we have all trespassed against ourselves and against life. None of us knew what he wanted from life, or, to be more precise, life didn't know what to do with us..."

"Eat sh—" de Coto began to object..

"Silence! I want peace and quiet."

"I'm not going to beat around the bush. Simply put: the accused are innocent, or, to be more precise, more innocent than the prosecutor, and the court, and the jury, and even more innocent than the defense."

Voices of protest.

"Fine, they did steal, and injure this man. But, ladies and gentlemen of the court, we don't really know, right, what drives someone to steal, to kill...?"

"To rape—" de Coto interrupted...

"—And to rape and...I request that the Illustrious Court remove those who keep yelping like this...And don't we know that there is no just verdict except the one you pronounce on yourself? Who among us does not admit his own sin to himself? Everybody admits it, Your Honor. We are all penitents, we have all passed judgment on ourselves, whether while asleep or awake, but who among us admits it when he's been justly convicted by God or other people or the devil? No one. We are the ones who know our own sins best, and the price we pay for them, and maybe we know our innocence best, too, but we do not, gentlemen, recognize other people's right to prescribe the gravity of our sins or to equate themselves with our conscience. Hence, if all of this is true, and if it is indeed we who are to know all of this most clearly, then we (or anybody else) could take upon ourselves the crime of the very pronouncement of some supposedly "objective" justice. But—" (here his tone became mocking) "—are we capable of judging a person, or a bird or a fly? We are not, gentlemen. We cannot judge so much as a bird, for its moral code belongs to it alone, and is understandable only to it, so even here we are helpless. No, gentlemen, we are not 'smarter' than a bird, or a wild beast, or even vermin, and we're not in a position to pass judgment on them. Not on a bird, nor mice, nor a cockroach."

"Get to the point!" Oleg heckled.

"As I said, gentlemen—not even mice. For, if we understand their nature, we will grasp that they are martyrs, just like we are, except that it is even harder for them, because their fate, embodied in a cat, does not permit the absurd hope to be born in their minds that they will someday overcome their destiny. Imagine, gentlemen, how we would feel if we managed to see the cat-incarnation of our fate? Well, anyway, let us return to the mice. They had no option (not even a degree of sensitivity, which would be absurd) other than a touch of cunning. ('Our privilege, gentlemen, is absurd!' he jeered.) They are, you know, a Gypsy-like band, only a little less free and happy. They will sing to you (and at night, while you're dreaming of freedom, while you are courting or frightening off your conscience, it is a poem and not squealing), and they will dance for you so that you're entertained and can go to sleep (which is all you desire), and then they'll share your portion with you, taking no account of your selfishness...I beg you, Your Honor, to remember all the services Macuka has rendered on behalf of Cell 11. We raised her from childhood, and while she was yet a baby, so to speak, we played with her, sang with her, and grew jealous of each other on account of the capriciousness of her affections. She grew up with us like that, as living proof of the way time, the passage of which seemed lost on us, did indeed continue to march on, impalpably but certainly, and of the way it was still in a position to make something big out of something small by means of its imperceptible flow...We looked at how small she was—just yea big!—and we didn't believe she could grow; we didn't believe it for the simple reason that we wanted to believe it, as if it were living proof of the inaccuracy of our mistaken ideas about time. For we believed, naively, gentlemen, that time had stopped, and simultaneously we were seeking 'obvious proofs'"—once again he started to assume a mocking tone—"that would vanquish this error of ours...And then we called it hope, and 'proof' of a sort...We saw her when she was small, as I said, and now we see how she has grown (and how she has brought forward 'proof' that time did not stop), how she filled out and became the mother of two innocent (yes: innocent) children who together with her are cowering here in the dock. For shame, gentlemen! I shall repeat just this one thing: I wish it to be noted for the record, Your Honor, that the merits of the defendant Macuka, mother and citizen of this house, are of such nature and quantity that, although we are here because of some quite serious infractions, she should not be permitted to experience ingratitude. Rather—only honor, and respect. I am, Your Honor, too much moved to be able to continue."

Quiet applause. Hitler and de Coto were the only ones to continue sitting there with their arms crossed. Then they called the witnesses.

"Tomahawk. Witness," Hitler announced austerely after the guard had approached the bench.

"I swear to tell the truth and nothing but the truth," he repeated after the juror, keeping his right hand on the *Little Church Calendar for the Leap Year 19***.

35

"In the night between the 5th and 6th of August, of this year, at around 3 o'clock in the morning, I heard a scream coming from #11. I ran over and peered in. I saw de Coto binding his shorter leg with a handkerchief—with that one there—and I heard him cursing the mouse-god that thought them up, and he was vowing to annihilate them even if he had to turn into a cat to do it. The others were laughing, especially Asclepius...The next night, at almost the same time, I heard shrieks and squeals coming from #11. And I recognized the voice of the defendant, Macuka. Then I was summoned by the plaintiff, de Coto, and he showed me, exultantly, the mess kit Macuka had been caught in. Then he stuck a piece of glass under the mess kit, and twisted it. The others told him to leave her alone. That's when the quarrel broke out. The defendant and Asclepius nearly came to blows. When I admonished them not to make a racket, Asclepius told me to judge whose side justice was on. So then I stated that I am only a guard and that a judgment will be forthcoming only from the court. To that Asclepius said: 'If that's the way it is, then you can be an eyewitness.' I agreed...Yes. But later—and the plaintiff himself related this to me—the children of the defendant Macuka, whose names I do not know (Old Asclepius fabricates the oddest names for everyone), came over to the mess kit and de Coto caught them by hand, because, he said, they didn't even resist." Thus spoke Tomahawk.

The jurors then whispered a bit amongst themselves and withdrew into the corner. There they continued whispering; they squabbled a bit, before finally returning to their places. Everyone sat there in silent anticipation. Hitler started writing something, and then got to his feet. Gavro and Oleg stood up also. Hitler then read aloud, in a voice both solemn and severe, that (according to section such-and-such, and paragraph this or that of the criminal code) Macuka and her children were sentenced to death.

In the cell, voices of protest were heard. De Coto was the only one who looked to be satisfied. Along with the judges, of course. At which point de Coto limped up to the podium and retrieved his boot and handkerchief. Then Hitler said unexpectedly:

"The court has determined that the execution must be carried out within twenty-four hours by Mr. De Coto. No objections will be considered."

"He's an expert at that," exclaimed Asclepius.

"Boo! Hangman!"

"There's no way!" De Coto said. "I am the plaintiff. I protest. I object. Let the court appoint someone else. How about, let's say, Asclepius. He's an authority on women. Who's ever seen the plaintiff—"

"The objection is overruled," Hitler said. "The court has had its say." He rose to his feet. After him, Gavro and Oleg stood up too. And after them, the others.

*

De Coto hesitated. The others stood next to him, pretending to dab their eyes. The water running from the faucet covered up the guard's steps. De Coto was standing between Hitler and Asclepius. Then, when he couldn't stand the torment any longer, de Coto pulled a can from his pocket and tossed it out into the tank. They watched Macuka wiggle and squirm and puff herself up. Then she sank, letting out a cry as she did so. Then they saw her go belly up. They waited some more. So de Coto took out another tin can and threw the mice into the water. Then the others put on their shirts and went out in lockstep. De Coto was the last to leave.

(1959)

THE SHOES

My shoes, which were lying there next to one another like
two animals, all of a sudden became radically elongated
and lost their shape; they took on the look of those objects
we look at every day for years but then unexpectedly, for
no reason whatsoever, as the saying goes, perceive with
wonderment, as if we were regarding them for the first
time. Nonetheless this feeling of seeing an object for the
first time neither surprised nor frightened me; I had
experience in this sort of thing and it came to my aid. Thus
I remember a cash register in the bistro that I frequented
in the evenings for year. If someone were to ask me not
how the cash register looks but whether a cash register is
even to be found on those premises, I'd answer either in
the negative or with a shrug of my shoulders. And so one
evening—it was in the fall—waiting for Lilijan, who had
said she was probably going to be a little late, I, after a wait
of almost forty-five minutes, ducked inside the bistro
(which had been consciously chosen as the site of our
meetings, so that in the case of inclement weather I could
take shelter or—something I'd never confess to Lilijan—
so that, in the event that she didn't turn up, I could drop in
there as into purgatory) and take a seat in one of the
corners after ordering a double cognac. And then, having
gotten my mind around the thought that she wouldn't be
coming that evening, tormented by jealousy and
uncertainty, my mind would start to "grasp at straws" and
my glance would begin to linger on the objects around me.
At first, this would happen, to all appearances, without the

conscious involvement of my mind, which was preoccupied with things of considerably greater importance than a run-of-the-mill steel cash register, but in fact my gaze was empty, and I would soon realize that it was much more lucid and meaningful than the carefree glances with which I took in the little café in the hours I spent breathlessly waiting for Lilijan. So all at once, no matter that I was completely wrapped up in thoughts of her, I noticed, via an auxiliary stream of awareness, that I was actually seeing that old-fashioned steel cash register for the first time. The reliefs on the nickeled lid in the shape of a kettledrum and a frieze gave its entire steel construction the appearance of a cathedral. That thought began to intrigue me, and if the presence of nightmare and suffering did not disappear or attenuate during that time, I did still comprehend abruptly that the "discovery" of this cash register-cathedral was simply a consequence of the alienation of my mind, which was approaching, in a moment of agitation, objects of which it had not before then taken note in its self-absorption but which now imposed themselves on it, all at once, as a necessity, like a place of asylum or a shell. After all, there was no necessity in it, except perhaps the fact that my spirit, in a moment of weakness, would latch onto an object as vulgar as an old-fashioned cash register. Experience told me that in all of this, however, there was nothing strange, for it had also often happened to me in the past that a face that I was used to seeing every day and found interesting I would catch sight of in a similar manner, after looking its way for a long time, in a moment when I was uninterested and, shall we say, absent.

So it was now (to return to the thing I'm telling you about), at dusk, in a ray of opaque moonlight, that I beheld with astonishment my own shoes, as if for the first time I was seeing something the significance and purpose of which I did not grasp. In those days I lived in a garret and would daydream, lying on the floor in my threadbare clothes, about Paris, and about the books I would write, where my history and my life today would experience the grace of being given form. That little room under the eaves had some sort of wondrous, well-nigh magical power of distortion. At night, by the light of my little lamp, like in the light of dusk and moonshine, my thoughts underwent an odd transformation, just as the objects in the room did: they all became unreal shapeless.

The detail that has made me digress from the subject at hand is the fact that I slept on the floor in those days. This is not without importance to this process of distortion. For, lying on the floor, I saw the things around me from a perspective that fundamentally changed their appearance. Thus I could look at a chair as if it were hanging down from the low ceiling, and the window looked like it belonged to an imaginary upper story; in other words, I saw everything from a worm's-eye view, which allowed objects to take on a superior and almost brutal appearance and attitude to me. My shoes cast long shadows as if they were "standing on tip-toes," although I could clearly tell that I was looking at them from the side. But this curious pair of animals was not the same size, and I didn't think any kind of optical illusion was in play here because they were lying there side by side. But they varied in size to the same degree that males of some species of animals differ from the females;: one held its head up, as if keeping watch, and the second one, half a length behind the first, had a serene look about it. Suddenly, however, I wanted to believe that those were two black cats, whose presence tormented me. For they did not rest, but rather came sneaking towards me with eyes as burnished and sharp as a razor. And yet their cautious approach did not in any way lessen the distance between us. Well, I finally had to assure myself that these were simply my shabby shoes. But at the same time I had to convince myself of the fact that I was just now experiencing them for the first time, and doing so above all as beings rather than as objects, and as animals, to boot, with which I had no connection. I endeavored with all my might to see myself in that nearly formless, grayish-black heap, my features, any kind of relation at all that would bring them closer to me. I was only able to recall that I'd bought them not so long ago (although I had worn them out quickly, dragging myself around run-down parts of town by day, and even more often by night, in search of sensations) and that they rubbed and squeezed my feet something awful until I improvised a solution to my torture by means of some deft cutting; I made a slit by using a razor-blade to make two diagonal incisions on each of the shoes, and this freed me from the tightness around my toes, where there were calluses. That moment brought home to me the fact that I had actually been, since the first instant, since our first encounter, in a state of hostilities with these shoes. Perhaps one could even say since before our first meeting. For now the very thought of purchasing new shoes called forth from me both discomfort and dread, for I had already experienced the way they vexed me continuously, like boots from the Spanish Inquisition, and the way they always left the skin of my heels covered in blood. But when I thought seriously about it, I felt I was being unjust and vengeful. Because I could have remembered, had I wanted to, some nice moments, too— if I had been inclined to disown them.

I had bought them suddenly for some reason, without mentioning anything to Lilijan about my intention to purchase new footwear. The truth is, she pretended that there was no shame in going out with me when I was unshaven and wearing shoes that looked like Charlie Chaplin's (on the contrary, she said that she liked it, since her father thinks I'm a painter, which must have flattered her) but she could never talk me into going with her to the theater or concerts. None of my proofs could ever persuade her that I could not go to the theater or concert "in this state"—referring above all to my shoes. She would then begin to reproach me for not wanting to go to the

41

concert *because of her*, while I said only that I could not go *with her*, but alone...

"I was afraid you would buy the ones with round tips, because I know you don't like the pointed ones. But these are nice. Tomorrow we are going to the theater. I want to see *No Exit*," she said happily, looking down immediately at my new shoes and trying to say everything in one breath, as if she were saying something that was self-evident: that we would be going to the theater.

"I'm going to carve them," I told her, just as calmly as could be. "I'm going to give them a C-section. I can't stand it anymore." Of course she opposed this with might and main, as if it were a matter of life and death, because she saw that I was quite capable of doing it. So that's how our break-up occurred back then, with her claiming that I was doing it just so I'd have an excuse for not taking her out to the play...

Thus I began to call to mind all the moments that had in some way ever tied me to the shoes that were now standing there, slanted, above me, throwing their long, bizarrely twisted shadows on the floor. And at last I made up my mind, after managing to remember my many walks with Lilijan, when I would roam along the Danube with her, through the coffee houses of the outlying districts where we danced a few rowdy calypsos amidst crowds of working girls and young toughs; our embraces in that cold garret, where we'd leave our shoes in a heap without cutting on the light so we could give ourselves to each other, breathlessly, in mute caresses; how we, when the clock on the town hall had sounded the hour for her departure, would hunt for our shoes in the pile and feel our way hastily through the darkness, and so on—I decided then that I would get to my feet and turn on the light so as to make a charcoal drawing of these monstrous shoes, which had become all at once a world unto themselves, a world that was indeed distant and distorted, but which—voilà—can be approached and conceptualized by the deployment of effort and desire. The Van Gogh-like drawing of mine in charcoal was supposed to play the role of intermediary, rendering intelligible to me these shoes that at the outset came across as unfamiliar, dangerous, and alien, but then, after I succeeded in connecting them in my memory to Lilijan again, drew near to me, as if someone had traipsed across the world of remembrances in them. This, then, was the method I wanted to use to preserve them from oblivion, to embalm them by means of this drawing, like the relics of a saint or the hand of a martyr who died for his or her ideals, because it all at once became obvious to me that on them rests an entire world, dozing dreamily; and this dark room of mine under the eaves, and my wanderings with Lilijan on the other side of the tracks, and everything that together with these shoes will go off to the city dump, if I do not pull it all out of the path of oblivion.

Therefore I stood up, sleepy, confused, in order to prepare the paper and charcoal and begin the embalming. Wearing my old rags, with my army blanket wrapped around my shoulders, like a sorcerer from some savage clan donning his vestment, I switched on the flickering light and approached my shoes as if they were the Host. Regarded from above, they looked miserable—dirty and ragged, misshapen and as tattered as two corpses picked apart by birds. So I picked them up, guardedly, with two fingers—but I let them go again immediately and shuddered to my very core. A rat came sliding out of one of the shoes, and with its long dirty tail it described an imaginary diagonal across the room from corner to corner, before making its way into a hole and erasing, in one fell swoop, everything that had wanted to escape oblivion.

(1960)

43

THE ROBOT

No one was surprised by his arrival. There was nothing miraculous about seeing a robot walk in through the door, choose a table, push away chairs, and study the menu. He did all of it as adroitly and matter-of-factly as any other guest would. With his finger he indicated the Wiener Schnitzel, and the waiter, not upset in the least, brought it to him. The robot skillfully cut up the meat into rather large pieces (knife in his right hand and fork in the left), poured wine into his glass, salted his food, broke the loaf of bread with his hands and popped morsels into his mouth, all with a rhythm that betrayed routine and a sense of propriety. There was nothing unusual in any of it. Not even in the fact that he then wiped off his steel lips with a fine white paper napkin. He wasn't going to request sandpaper just because his lips are made of steel!

The only unusual thing was that he drank an entire bottle of wine after dinner. And then another one. He politely sent back the soda water that the waiter brought with the second liter. Obviously something was not right with him. This was clear to all who knew him well, especially when he tossed the fifth liter down his steel gullet.

Little by little a sense of doubt came over the waiter. He communicated his anxiety to the manager, who merely shrugged his shoulders. "But what if he gets drunk?" the waiter whispered excitedly. The manager thought about it for a moment and then responded: "But it's a robot. A

44

garden-variety robot!" So the waiter calmed down and took the robot his sixth liter of wine.

The robot, however, began draining his glasses at one go: the seventh liter, the eighth, the ninth. His eyes were rolling drunkenly, and his head bobbed from side to side, but when they started to play "No such thing as lucky in love" he smashed a glass on the floor. A lady close to where the glass landed started to protest: "Insolence. They should throw him out and give him twenty-five lashes so he learns a little decorum." Nonetheless he continued to drink, failing to take the protests of the guests into account. Later he apologized to the waiter, in written form of course: "Dear Sirs," read his message, printed in crude block letters, "I beg the pardon of your esteemed company, especially the lady whom I inadvertently doused. I would be infinitely grateful to you if you would allow me to join your society, for loneliness is killing me. Sincerely, your devoted…" etc. The esteemed company read the robot's message with great interest and then began its consultations. Some of them said, "Why shouldn't we accept him into our society? He seems to be a good-natured fellow and it looks like he's unhappy." The others said: "Loneliness?! But it's just an run-of-the-mill robot. He might create unpleasantness for us and land us in trouble. Everybody would be staring at us." And the third group: "He must have money out the arse. He can pick up the tab!" But the lady declared: "I won't sit at the same table as a cold, insensate creature like that robot. He is of a lower race, somewhere between blacks and Jews."

Thus they refused, out of chivalry, to accept him into their company. It was out of caution that they passed their decision along to him via the waiter, asking that he (of course) not get angry and also accept their apology. They also turned down, very politely, the drinks he had ordered for them. Whereupon the robot ordered himself a tenth liter of wine. The waiter looked at him with amazement and fright in his eyes. This robot had never before drunk more than seven or eight liters of wine. Never. Not even at New Year's. Once again the waiter communicated his fear to the manager. The manager thought about it for a moment, then grew serious and declared: "Take him the bill and don't give him another drop to drink. If he balks—throw him out."

The waiter returned and informed the robot that it was closing time and drinks were no longer being served. The robot glanced at his watch and then rolled his eyes around to the waiter and held a bottle out to him, apparently demanding that someone bring him another drink. Embarrassed, the waiter shrugged his shoulders: "There's no more, sir. We don't serve intoxicated guests."

At that point something snapped in the robot. Like when a clock stops. With a deliberate angular motion he raised the bottle with his right hand and smashed it over the waiter's head. The society lady said to her cavalier: "You see, I told you we shouldn't accept him into our society. Heaven forbid, he might've struck you." A fanfare sounded as two policemen appeared in the doorway and approached the table at which the robot sat with its head plunged in its hands. "Get up!" shouted the one of the policeman, shaking him by the shoulder. The robot didn't budge. Then they took hold of him, one from one side and the other from the other side, and stood him on his feet. At that moment the manager came running up and said that the robot hadn't paid yet. One of the policemen pressed a button on his steel rump marked "Cash," and out fell a silver coin. "How much?" he asked the manager. Without missing a beat, the manager replied, "One hundred fifty-five." The policeman kept hitting the button, but the mechanism grew disobedient at ninety-six. They were unable to extract even one additional dinar. "What's wrong with you?" The policeman inquired of the manager. "Why have you gotten so pale?" In the meantime the manager, looking petrified, had sat down on a chair. "Nothing," he said. "Just this air." He drained a glass of water. "Nothing, you see? Nothing. This damned air. We need to open a window."

The robot left between the policemen, his head hanging, his step uncertain. When he reached the door, he stopped all of a sudden, grabbed the policemen, and with one powerful move tossed them out. All of this happened rapidly and unexpectedly.

By now the guests were frightened. One of the ladies started screaming. Someone shouted desperately into the phone: "Hello? Hello?" But the robot remained standing at the door, rolling his bloodshot eyes around the room. A tense silence prevailed. But all of a sudden he turned around and hurriedly walked out. He nearly fell when he tripped over the threshold.

The customers sat there for a long time, confused and helpless. No one dared open the door and go outside. The waiter whom the robot had struck with a bottle reappeared with a white turban on his head. He was holding a revolver in his hand. "I'm going out there," he said in a voice that sounded like suicide. And he moved with decisive strides towards the door, his revolver cocked and ready.

At that moment the musicians again played a flourish in order to drown out the business at hand. The guests weren't supposed to witness unpleasant scenes and bloody showdowns. All eyes were fixed on the door.

Suddenly, as if by command, the music ceased. All that could be heard was muffled breathing. The waiter with the white turban on his head was standing on the threshold, heroically erect and looking mysterious. Then he thrust his revolver into his pocket, and his voice filled the void of anticipation: "Come see, gentlemen!" There was a sneer in his voice: "It's just an ordinary robot. A drunken robot!"

The guests, or the boldest among them, hurried to the door.

Propped on his arms against the wall, with his legs spread wide and his head bowed low, the robot was— vomiting.

(1961)

THE BOY WITH A BIRD
ON
HIS SHOULDER

The boy who sat in the first bench, and who was known as Andreas Sam, or Andi for short, didn't know how to weave baskets out of twigs. Nor did he know how to weave baskets from straw, or even of cattails, the way the little girls did. He didn't know how to make either handles for axes or handles for hoes; in all his days he had never even made a handle for a hammer. In other words, he didn't know how to make anything, and his hands were as white as the hands of a young girl. And he didn't know what to do with them. Because everyone kept looking at them. Everyone. And they were unused hands, like white silk gloves that get worn only once.

"What do you know how to make?" the teacher asked him. And she looked down at his hands. Everyone looked at his hands. For a moment they all stopped weaving their twig baskets.

"Nothing," he said.

"You'll learn how," the teacher said. "Watch how the others are doing it."

"Yes," he said. "I'll learn how."

He began to observe Lacika, whose reddened fingers were braiding together the flexible willow branches like ten knitting needles. Laci stuck out his tongue at him, and Andi blushed across his whole face.

49

"You have white hands," Laci sneered in a whisper.

"Yes," he said.

"And you don't know how to make anything," Laci said.

"Actually I do," he said.

"Teacher!" Laci called out. "He says he does know how to make something."

"What is it that you know how to make, Sam?" the teacher asked then. "Don't be shy."

"Airplanes," he said.

They all looked once more at his hands, and the teacher continued:

"Airplanes?"

"Yes," he said. "They can fly, too."

"Very well," the teacher replied. "What do you need in order to do that?"

"Paper," he said. "Two pages you tear out of a notebook. One for the wings, and the other for the tail.

"Fine," said the teacher. "Come up here so I can give it to you."

Once again they all stopped working on their baskets. They were looking at his hands. Then he started to fold the paper that the teacher had given him. He made some triangles, and he made some pleated boxes that looked like snapdragons. Then he cut out the tail with its large stabilizer and took a red pencil out of his box. He drew crosses on the wings and tail. Symmetrical ones.

"What are those?" Laci asked him.

"The markings," he said. "Every plane has its own markings." He pressed down one more time on the creases in the wings, bent them a little bit, and spit on the plane for good luck, and then he threw it into the air and let out a "Rrrr." The plane began to fly like a sea-gull, brushing the black sea of the chalkboard with its wing, looping around Emőke Szabó's head, and landing obediently on the boy's shoulder.

"Rrrr...rrrr," he repeated.

They were all looking at him.

"What does it mean when you go 'rrrr'"? Laci wanted to know.

"That's the motor," he said.

"Get on with your work," the teacher interrupted. "After class Sam can show you how to make airplanes."

"Me first," Laci cried. "You and I sit on the same bench."

"OK," he said. "But don't stick your tongue out at me any more."

"All right," said Laci. "I'll share my lunch with you."

"This plane is mine," Andreas said. "I'll make you a different one."

And he thought of how Laci would be giving him half of his food every day, while he made airplanes for him. His stomach began to quiver with happiness.

At recess two planes took off. One of them fell to earth near the fountain and the boys there tore it to pieces. The other one flew up very high and, caught by the wind, disappeared beyond the trees and rooftops.

"It turned into a bird!" yelled an astonished Emőke Szabó.

The next day at recess Lacika gave him half the food he had brought for snack, and the other boy showed him how to make planes that would land on your shoulder like a bird. Everyone gathered around and stood there as his fingers scuffed and slid along the paper. He had been biting his lips and tongue so much that they showed fiery red spots like the color he had used for the crosses.

During class, all the students kept their hands in their benches, tearing pages out of their notebooks. In the next break, whole squadrons of planes took off across the yard. Some of them got caught in the low-hanging branches of the apple tree, their tails fluttering like cuckoos, and others plummeted headfirst like suicidal doves that didn't know how to contradict their hearts. A third bunch fell into the damp lilac bushes.

Andreas had eaten half a slice of bread with lard, and on his lips were tiny crystals of sugar and a smile. The tail of the white airplane on his shoulder fluttered back and forth. Emőke Szabó had a little smile in her green eyes as she walked around flapping her skirt and scaring the chickens.

"Look at this," Laci said to him. "Rrrr! Rrrr!"

The airplane made a loop in the air and landed obediently on Laci's shoulder.

"It has markings, too," Laci added, showing him the swastika that looked like a black shape on a butterfly's wing. The other boy chuckled and kept searching for bits of sugar around his mouth. Then Lacika stuck out his tongue at him, a tongue stained with dark red spots.

The other boys laughed. The wind began to rock the paper on Andi's shoulder, and it blew the plane away. The boys stomped on it. When the bell rang, Andi was still standing there by the damp lilacs. He was trying to find the little grains of sugar around his lips. The taste on his tongue was sweet and salty.

(1962)

A BESTIARY

BUTTERFLIES

In the garden of Mr. Roth, our building superintendent, the apple trees were in bloom. Mr. Roth stood leaning on the fence, watching the way the butterflies mingled with the foam-like apple blossoms.

"If you hold it for too long in your hand, it won't be able to fly," he said to me.

"Do you mean, Mr. Roth, that I have to let it go?" I asked.

"Yes," he said. "I think it would be wise to refrain from tormenting it."

"Do you mean, Mr. Roth, that this hurts it?"

"Yes," he said. "Every living creature suffers."

"I guess you mean, Mr. Roth, that it hurts when I hold it by the wings?"

"Yes," Mr. Roth said. "That causes it pain."

"I guess you mean, Mr. Roth, that it has a heart and all the rest?"

"Yes," he said. "A heart and all the rest, like a person."

"All right," I said. "I'll let it go, but you have to tell me, Mr. Roth, why the butterfly can't talk then."

"It talks," Mr. Roth said. "It's just that we don't hear it."

"I guess you mean, Mr. Roth, that it's crying now?"

"It is certainly crying," he said. "Only you can't hear it."

At that point I spread apart my index finger and thumb, between which I'd been squeezing the butterfly.

"You're right, Mr. Roth," I said. "Here on my fingers you can still see its tears."

Sometime around then I began going to the bookstore in the next street. It was across from the pastry shop. The first time I went over there with Ana, and after that I went by myself. They had little color photographs for sale. Inside it was cool and it smelled of paper and glue, rubber and *eau de cologne*.

"Well, if isn't the little shrimp who collects butterflies," said the lady with the scent of walnut leaves. She helped me select a picture. And I fell in love with her because of that scent. I was afraid she'd notice, because I kept turning awfully red. She wore a black silk apron and had long red fingernails she'd run gently over my skin. But one day I got up the courage to say:

"I want to give you this Apollo. I hope you like it."

"Thank you, junior," she said, kissing me on the lips. Then she backed away and immediately started to laugh.

"Oh, look at the little man. Look how red he's getting...Good grief! Now he's going to cry!"

She gave me back the butterfly I had given her, and I rushed pell-mell out into the street.

At home I gave Ana the album with my butterfly collection and I got into bed without a word. My temperature had gone up to 102.

WORMS

Every day Mr. Roth brought worms in a tin container to his garden. He would walk up to the fence, and I knew he was going to open the lid on the container next and empty the worms out over the fence. Then he and I would chat, you know, as the opportunity and mood permitted. We'd also watch the worms disentangle themselves from their skein and disappear into the soil.

One day, completely by chance, because we didn't have anything else to talk about, I asked Mr. Roth why he planted worms.

"Cucumber plants grow from them," he said.

"Mr. Roth, I hope you don't believe—"

"Yes," he said. But seeing my doubts about what he was saying to me, he followed up with: "If you don't believe it, go ask your father."

"All right, Mr. Roth," I said. "I will check this out, because it seems doubtful to me. Very much so. How useful could a worm be, when it has no beginning and no end?"

I repeated my doubts to my father. He laughed, and my mother gave me a kiss, and Ana said I was extraordinarily stupid and everyone was going to make fun of me (next year) in school.

Mr. Roth laughed, too, as he asked me the next day:

"Well, what did I tell you, o wise one?...I suppose you're going to say that I was wrong?"

THE HART AND THE HIND

At first we rode on the little blue streetcar, and then we went on foot, past the marshy stretch. We usually went out on Sundays or holidays.

"Where shall we go today?" my mother would ask, as soon as we found ourselves in the street. Ana and I would agree that we wanted to go see the deer.

"Thank God," my mom would say. "Thank God the two of you see eye to eye for once. Just don't let there be any cries of 'Mama, carry me! Mama, carry me!' on the way."

I wouldn't say anything, even though that was meant for me. (Typically my legs would give out on me on the way back.) I wasn't sure that I could hold out, and I didn't want to fib. That's why I kept my mouth shut.

It was in the early fall. A thin mist had risen over the marsh past which we were walking. A somber-looking castle would appear before us, overgrown with wild vines, surrounded by a tall fence of iron bars. Here, in the yard of this castle that had been abandoned forever, the deer were known to graze or chew their cud in the shade.

We would stop at the fence, out of breath, hands stretched through the bars. At that point a hart would show up, his eyes huge and dark, and behind him would come a hind on her slender legs, with a dark moist spot at the end of her snout. They'd come up to the fence and eat sugar from my mother's hand.

Nothing is happening in this story, and nothing is going to happen. (On the way home my mother would carry me.) In this story there is actually no way back, and in this story the fellow usually known as Andreas, or simply Andi, isn't going to ask anything.

In this story my mother holds out two cubes of sugar on her open palm.

(1962)

THE END OF THE SUMMER

An Austro-Hungarian naval captain and amateur biologist noted once in his journal that he had seen an example of a rare and precious small butterfly, the *Belenois helcida,* the provenance of which is in Madagascar, in this area back in 1911. This bit of data remained unverified and suspect, even given the authority of this particular amateur biologist. But this was precisely the thing that had drawn Beljanski to Miločer to spend his vacation. He arrived there at the end of August, just as the tourist season was starting to wind down. In the hotel, besides him, there was only a married couple from Berlin and two English ladies, apparently spinsters. He was hoping to complete his doctoral thesis and, at the same time, prove the veracity of the captain's facts. But what he was looking for was close to being an *idée fixe,* even though he had pretty reliably verified the whole thing before committing himself to this search. He found the notation by the amateur biologist in a German study in which he had been browsing while on the hunt for data for his thesis on climate conditions and the distribution of butterflies. More or less involuntarily he had begun, a year earlier, collecting the literature on this, and he was still no closer to nailing down an exact topic, except insofar as it was going to have something to do with butterflies. The actual topic, then, was rather uninteresting, one of those things that a young person chooses in order to get out of work, or because the professor forces it on him. In addition, this subject was closer to esthetics than to biology. But there was in this

theme (butterfly: a flower and a bird) that he had chosen—
totally randomly, as it seemed to him—some deeper
determinism of which he himself was not even fully aware.
If he thought hard about it, he could barely, perhaps,
adduce from his childhood some experience that had
created in him a link to butterflies. He was five or six years
of age when he heard his father remark that butterflies live
for only one day. Naturally, that was an utterly insignificant
detail that could not have led him into the arms of his
current interests or his dissertation. He had already long
ago forgotten that minor sense of shock with which
children react to their first awareness of life and death.
Nothing else from his biography could justify the interest
in this slightly poetic subject, either. For Beljanski was to a
considerable extent a positivist, something that had
definitely attracted him to the exact sciences, which in turn
merely confirmed his attitudes toward life and the world. A
person is born, lives, and dies (unfortunately); plants give
off oxygen and humans breathe it in; and butterflies turn
into worms, just as humans do, after all. Only with
butterflies it's faster, more obvious.

Now, although he was on holiday, he was getting up
early and roaming around with his butterfly net. On
departing from the hotel and upon his return, he deftly
camouflaged the net by removing it from the pole and
hiding it in his pocket so that later, when he was some
distance away, he could remount it.

One day, upon returning to his hotel in the early
evening, he caught sight of a strange procession that had
suddenly emerged from a stand of pine trees not far away:
a man, a woman, and a child. There was something
unusual in their appearance, something that drew his
attention. The man, powerfully built and red-bearded,
sunburnt, was carrying on his shoulders the child—a girl
of five or six. She was clutching the man's hair, and her
legs dangled down his athletic chest. The woman was
walking along a step or two behind them. She was slender,

wearing a bathing suit the color of cherries, and her blonde hair, still wet, had something of the hues of the setting sun. What drew Beljanski's attention was not so much their beauty as the beauty of the scene: all at once they cropped up and then they vanished, without speaking, without any noise at all. Even though they had crossed within a few steps of the bush behind which he was standing, he hadn't heard a sound, not even the rustling of the pine branches that had opened and closed behind them. He thought that he would meet them over lunch in the hotel, but when he failed to see them there, he thought nothing more of them. Because the day wasn't suited for swimming in the sea, he remained in his room, paging through his notes and organizing them, before finally falling asleep.

When he awoke, the sun had already gone down (his room had a view to the west), and darkness had fallen and the air was somehow—suddenly and aromatically—autumnal. Beljanski lit a cigarette and started trying to recall the dream he'd had. He had dreamt he caught sight of that butterfly of his, the *Belenois helcida*. At first he'd thought it was a flower. Some flower that was unknown to him. Something like a pansy, half-yellow and half-white, with dark, almost black borders on the petals and a patch of the lightest pink in the middle, around the stamen. He wanted to go catch this *Belenois* (*madagascariensis*) at the spot where he remembered seeing it in his dream, but in vain, for it was already late in the day. The fake flower abruptly closed up its petals and lifted off, as if borne on the wind, towards the sea. Beljanski smiled: that stupid dream.

But then he got dressed and went out for a little stroll. He did not take his butterfly net with him, probably to prove to himself how free he was from superstition. Or because it would be truly laughable to do so at the end of September, in weather like this, at evening-time....He loitered a bit on the path leading to the beach, and then he made his way towards a village that lay two to three kilometers from the hotel.

All at once (and simultaneously) he got a glimpse of that strange couple with their child. They were walking along the sandy beach: the man (and the child), with the woman following a step or two behind. Their legs stabbed the sand without making a sound. They passed by him as if he were a stone wall. No, it couldn't be that they'd failed to see him. It was more as if they didn't want to see him. They were watching the setting Sun, as if they were praying to it, or as if they were under a spell. Involuntarily Beljanski turned to follow them, but the sea had already erased their tracks from the sand.

Returning to his hotel, Beljanski started thinking things over. What was this sublime sense of peace that seemed to carry them along? What about the rich stillness that enveloped them? Where'd they come from? And where were they lodging, actually? For apparently they weren't guests at the hotel, or else he would have to have seen them at lunch or some evening in the bar. Beljanski decided to go looking for them the following day, to spy on them. Not so much out of genuine curiosity, but for the sake of amusement sake, to pass the time.

The next day he began walking up and down the beach early in the morning; he climbed up to the neighboring villages at the base of the mountain...Nothing. All he discovered were those two English ladies—the spinsters who, shielded by boulders, were sunbathing in the nude in a small quarry. He quickly beat a hasty retreat and returned to his hotel, fatigued.

After lunch he had a nice long nap and awoke feeling refreshed, lively. Through the open window the aromatic freshness of the final days of summer made its way into his room, a placid quietness. Seemingly impelled by the calm, he unexpectedly recalled the curious strangers whom he had already put out of his mind. He got out of bed and went down to the bar. At the counter he had a *pelinkovac* and then left. He walked west, along the beach, barefooted. On the sand in front of those little village houses right by the shore, some children were lounging, rolling sluggishly about as if they were amphibians. Then he came to the limestone boulders that precipitously blocked off the sandy expanse. For a moment he hesitated; then he waded into the water. He had to cross a narrow tongue of it in order to get to the bluffs. Up onto the rocks he clambered, where he clung to the hot, fractured face of the limestone. The rock was painfully rough and looked rusty, splotched with yellow-green algae and lichens, which looked like they'd been gnawed at. Somewhere in the heart of the stone, water was slapping rhythmically and growling, giving off hollow and muffled echoes as in a cave. He listened intently to the hot pulse of the stone, the great heart of the sea, and then stood up and tried to go on. But all at once he halted and pressed himself once more to the face of rock. On the beach encircled by boulders and consisting of small, flat white pieces of quartz, similar to pieces of hard candy that had been sucked on for a long time, the strange little girl was sitting; until now she had always been a whole head or two higher than him, seated as she usually was upon the shoulders of her red-bearded father. She sat now by herself on the shore, more like a bird than child, somehow oddly white, transparent. Leaning back on her arms, with her head a little turned to the side, and her face toward the sun, she seemed to be contemplating something: this wasn't a little amphibian like the other children he had seen earlier on the sand. This was more like a bird, a winged bug or a bee, a butterfly.

Bjelinski stood there above her, close enough that he could see her lowered eyelashes. He set about searching with his eyes for the others whom he was used to seeing with her. He strained his ears, but caught only the splashing of the sea somewhere in the limestone. Then he quietly withdrew and carefully, as if he were studying the stone, started to go around to verify that of which he was almost certain: that the little girl's parents were somewhere in the vicinity. But there was nothing. Only the stillness of the sun's descent and the noise of the sea. He quickly turned around and starting backing down the sharp stone, because it occurred to him that she was capable of...of disappearing all of a sudden, flying away. He began to hurry to so much—frightened by the prospect of it—that he barked his shin. He paid no attention, however, to the pain, which was inconsequential.

The girl was still sitting there, motionless. She had merely lowered and turned her head a little (as with those flowers that turn to follow the sun). She abruptly opened her eyes and saw him up above. She didn't budge but looked him straight in the eyes, curious, smiling. He didn't dare to do anything but stay rooted to the spot. He could not even ask her anything. When he caught sight of a heap of little stones next to her, carefully selected, he walked across the sand and took her several pieces of quartz and a shell. The girl clapped her hands a few times, picked up the stones, and laid them in her lap. Then she said something, in a language completely unfamiliar to him, and started to pick through more of the small rocks around her. She tossed some of them into the sea while placing others on the stack at her side. Then she squeezed her hands between her knees and shrugged her shoulders, looking in his direction as if to say: what shall we do now?

"Inge! Inge!" He started when he heard these words from behind his back. Above him stood the red-bearded man and the woman, whose eyes told him she was the girl's mother. Beljanski wanted to say something, to strike up a conversation with them, but they appeared not to have noticed him.

All he grasped was that they had not come along the beach but had burst forth from the sea; they were dripping water and their hair was wet. Beljanski nonetheless mumbled something, probably "Good day," in English, but still neither one took any notice of him: they were standing there lost in contemplation of the setting sun. Then the man quietly lifted the little girl onto his shoulders, placing her legs around his neck, and strode out into the water. First the man, and after him the woman. Beljanski stood there as if bewitched. He watched as they disappeared in the distance and the gold of their hair mixed with the liquid gold of the sun. When they were lost to view, he climbed hysterically to the top of the tallest of the boulders and began to scan the open sea for them. In the distance a gull was circling, cawing. The sea was peaceful and empty as far as his eye could see.

(1967)

AN AMERICAN STORY

His name was John. J,O,H,N. He had a surname just like that, too, totally ordinary, Yankee: Smith. His little pug nose was freckled, and he had reddish hair and dark blue eyes on account of which *Miss* Smith, his maternal aunt, called him *Blue Violet* when he was little.

"Now why is my Blue Violet so sad?" Miss Smith would ask him when he came home from school pouting. His eyes were covered by the large bill of a cricket cap on which the word *Massachusetts* was written in gaudy red letters. That was the name of the club that John rooted for, because his older brother Alec played for them.

And John would answer, without pushing the cap up from his eyes so that Aunt Mary wouldn't notice his tears, because Johnny was a very short-tempered and disdainful little brat:

"Nothing. It's nothing."

"Then why doesn't my Violet want to eat lunch?"

"No reason. It's nothing."

"Then why won't my Little Blue Violet admit that he doesn't know how much seven times seven is, or twenty-seven minus eighteen? Why won't he admit that he doesn't know where the headwaters of the Mississippi are?"

Johnny, however, just sat at the table and said nothing; he was not going to permit the sun to dry the dew from his eyelashes. He no longer answered in the negative; he wasn't saying anything at all. He was a proud little urchin, and it was only to his mom that he confessed when he had something to confess. That's why he was silent now.

Johnny, a.k.a. *Blue Violet*, waited for his mom to come home from work.

Then, when his mom was home from work, he began, "Mom—"

"Oh, Johnny dear?"

And they understood each other right away.

"—Mrs. Morgan punished me because I slugged that sneak Horace Greenwood in the nose really hard. She told me that I had to tell you. That she gave me a severe reprimand. And that you have to go talk with her tomorrow or some other time before vacation starts."

Johnny Smith was quite and insolent and candid little brat. That's why he told his mother everything he was supposed to. After that, he whipped the cap off of his head, the way his older brother had done when he still lived at home, and began to slurp the soup that had already grown cold.

At that point, Mrs. Smith, his mother, inquired of him: "*Johnny dear*, did he call you that name again? That thing about you being—"

"*Yes, mother*," Johnny said, but I can't stand it any longer. I just can't understand why he calls me that. That's why I came back at him with:

> *prove it*
> and he said
> *look at your pupils*
> then I told him
> *you're lying*
> *see for yourself*

then I went off to the bathroom, and in the mirror I saw that Horace was not lying. When I went back to the classroom, I felt as if I were going to cry. Then I looked right at Horace Greenwood and I saw that his pupils were black, too. That's when I realized that he was picking on me, and so that's why I popped him one on the snout as soon as Miss Morgan stepped out. Because I realized that he wasn't telling me the truth. He did not tell me why they call me that. The thing with my eyes was just teasing."

Johnny was a hard-headed little imp, and that's why he added: "I will fight every one of them until they quit calling me that. Why have they given me that name?"

Mrs. Smith, his mom, caressed his head gently but also admonished him a bit with these words:

"*Johnny dear, Johnny dear*, how long will we go on like this?"

One day Johnny's brother Alec, however, explained to him what it was really about. Johnny was only twelve and had already been expelled from school. So Alec said this to him:

"Johnny, things can't go on like this. You'll never be a man, for crying out loud! If you continue to…You're not a violet; you're a *Woolf*, a little wolf."

"But why do I have that nickname? If you tell me, then I'll give you my word of honor that I'll never hit anyone else."

"But Johnny—you're a crybaby."

"All right, then I'll start fights. I'll turn into Joe Louis."

"But why Joe Louis, Johnny?"

"He's strong. The strongest."

"He's black."

"He's the strongest."

"But you aren't black."

So then Johnny added:

"No matter, Alec. I'LL BECOME BLACK."

"And if I tell you why they call you 'Nigger'? What will you turn into then?"

"Whatever you want. I'll enroll in college."

"Should I really tel you?"

"If you know then tell me. Otherwise, Alec, I'm going to take a bite out of your ear."

"Well, well. Look at you."

"Out with it, Alec."

"How am I supposed to tell you, Johnny, you crybaby? OK. Here goes. One of your grandfathers, actually your grandfather's grandfather, had negro blood through one of his grandfathers. So there. That's why. That's the reason they call you that. Everybody in town knows about it...But you, Johnny, are a big wimp, and I never knew how to explain it all to you...Well, it could happen—note that I'm saying 'could'—that your son will be that way, too. A darkie."

"*Thank you, Alec,*" Johnny responded. "I get it. I will finish school and enroll in college. You'll see. Johnny keeps his word, even though you say he's a big sissy. You'll see, Alec."

Johnny was not a crybaby. And he kept his word. He nearly outstripped Alec. Alec explained it away by saying he was always busy with cricket and rugby, but this response was not justified in the least, since Johnny trained as a boxer and still took his law degree after four years. Just one semester behind Alec, even though Alec was three years older.

After that he moved to the South and opened up a legal practice. He quickly acquired a reputation as an expert on the problems of black people. He published several highly regarded pamphlets on the segregation of the races in the South, and he led a delegation to President Roosevelt that managed to win some very significant changes to government regulations, including—but not limited to—recognition of the right of black children to receive an education.

In his thirtieth year he married a black woman who worked in his practice as a law clerk. Mrs. Smith could thank none other than "Dr." Smith for her emancipation. And he couldn't have done his job without her.

On his thirty-third birthday, three years after their wedding, John Smith mentioned to his wife that he didn't feel well. The night before, at a reception in honor of a visiting delegation from Alabama, he had probably eaten something that didn't agree with him. These damned allergies had hounded him since his college days. Earlier, he'd been excused from work for three months on account of them, and he'd also had an exemption form military service, since he was allergic to the uniform and it left his body covered in dark blotches. As soon as he switched to his lightweight workout clothes, the splotches disappeared overnight, so to speak. Nevertheless, they thought now was a good time to contact Dr. Matthews.

When the doctor arrived, John Smith was just lying there, drenched in perspiration. On his body he had some odd dark splotches, and the whites of his eyes had grown yellow and turbid, things that Dr. Matthews interpreted as symptoms of a kind of contagious jaundice that was fairly widespread among the black population but quite rare among whites.

Dr. Matthews wrote out a prescription and reassured Mrs. Smith. He recommended rest and a strict diet for her husband. As he was leaving, Dr. Matthews added, in an offhand manner: "You should have called me earlier. Now I fear that the treatment is going to take a while."

"But Johnny only fell ill this morning," said Mrs. Smith. "Last night he was still completely fine, and in a great mood."

Dr. Matthews thought for a moment and then promised that he would come by again the next day. Should the patient be doing poorly in the meantime, his wife should summon him sooner. Regardless of the time of day. He would spare no effort in treating Mr. Smith.

Early the next morning, at about four o'clock, Dr. Matthews was awakened by the telephone.

"Okay," said the doctor, standing up uncertainly but without removing the receiver from his ear. "I'll come right away."

Mrs. Smith wasn't joking: John Smith, whom they had called "Blue Violet" at home and "Nigger" at school (when he was a little boy up north), was lying there, smiling. He was drenched in perspiration but was apparently cured.

Dr. Matthews had to sit down so that he did not betray his astonishment. John Smith, whom the people down there in the South called "Dr." Smith, had turned into a black man overnight. He died that same day and was buried, with full municipal honors, in the "black" graveyard. It was his wish to be taken here. The entire African-American South mourned for him. The well-known Louis Armstrong played some blues for him at the funeral.

The final words of the deceased, spoken into the ear of the good Dr. Matthews, were symptomatic of a man who'd had a mental breakdown. Naturally enough, Dr. Matthews guarded the secret with professional discretion. Confident that no one would doubt his report about a heart attack due to a genetic defect and stress at work, Dr. Matthews did not reveal his inability to confirm the real symptoms accompanying this unusual illness and unusual death. He himself was satisfied with the rather general assertion—actually the claim was just a few dim intimations—that there are some conditions and phenomena that operate beyond the framework of the material world. One day, though, when every possible piece of evidence of his helplessness had truly dematerialized, Dr. Matthews made use of an appropriate occasion to pose a question to Mrs. Smith: Was she acquainted with anyone named Horace Greenwood? She answered, however, that she'd never even heard the name before. This only confirmed the doctor's suspicion that the late John Smith had been mentally disturbed. For here's what he had said that day:

"That stupid Horace Greenwood is to blame for everything!"

This was, as we've said, a confirmation of his hunch. And it eased his conscience, of course.

(1967)

NB: *Translator's note*: Words appearing in this translation in italics were italicized and written in English by Kiš in the original. The word that Kiš uses for an African-American is *crnja*, which has an altogether harsher connotation than the standard word for "black man," which is *crnac*.

Printed in Dunstable, United Kingdom